Charlotte Jane Battles Bedtime

Myra Wolfe

Illustrated by Maria Monescillo

HARCOURT CHILDREN'S BOOKS

Houghton Mifflin Harcourt

Boston   New York

The illustrations in this book were done in watercolor with digital retouching and use of textures.

The text type was set in Fifteen 36.

The display type was hand-lettered by Dia Calhoun.

LIBRARY OF CONGRESS CATALOGING-IN-PUBLICATION DATA

Wolfe, Myra.

Charlotte Jane the Hearty battles bedtime! / written by Myra Wolfe ; illustrated by Maria Monescillo.

p. cm.

Summary: From the day Charlotte Jane was born on a pirate ship she has had "formidable oomph," but when she succeeds in conquering sleep by staying up all night, her oomph seems to weigh anchor.

ISBN 978-0-15-206150-0

[1. Sleep—Fiction. 2. Pirates—Fiction. 3. Parent and child—Fiction.] I. Monescillo, Maria, ill. II. Title.

PZ7.W8196Ch 2011

[Fic]—dc22

2010043398

Manufactured in the U.S.A.

WOZ 10 9 8 7 6 5 4 3 2

4500333195

For my wildly delightful children: Sophie, James, and Theodore —M.W.
For Noa, who was born at the same time as this story's art —M.M.

HARLOTTE JANE THE HEARTY came
howling into the world with the sunrise.
"Arr. She's finer than a ship full of jewels,"
said her mother, smiling.
"Arr," agreed her father.
"Also," said her mother, "she's got oomph."
"*Formidable* oomph," said her father.

They were right.
Her first words came early.

EN GARDE!

Her first steps came late.

She relished swashbuckling sessions,

treasure hunts,

and Fantastic Feats of Daring.

"I like to get all the juice out of my days!"
she would say.

And bedtime was not juicy.

"Sleep is your friend, little doubloon," said her father.

"No one can be hearty without it," said her mother.

Charlotte Jane did not agree.

She began to go to bed later . . .

and later . . .

and later . . .

until one dark night she didn't go to bed at all.

"Victory!" she whispered into the morning.

But Charlotte Jane did not feel hearty. Her oomph seemed to have gone to sleep without her.

"Traitor," she said. "A good plate of cackle fruit will jostle you up." It didn't.

Neither did a swashbuckling session with One-Eyed Tom.

Or a treasure hunt.

And she was too sapped to even
think of Fantastic Feats of Daring.

Her parents were worried.

"What's the matter?" asked her mother.

"Aye, sweet pomegranate, tell us," said her father.

"Arr," said Charlotte Jane. "My oomph's weighed anchor."

This would not do.

A hunt for the missing oomph began.

"It's not in the closet,"
said her mother.

"It's not in the bathtub!"
called her father.

"It's not in the fridge!"
her mother shouted.

"It's not in the garden!"
her father bellowed.

Charlotte Jane dragged herself
up to her room and looked
out the window.
There was her mother,
digging through
the neighbor's recycling bin.
There was her father,
climbing the old oak tree.

And there was her featherbed.

Charlotte Jane gave it a fearsome glare.

Bedtime was not juicy. Sleep was for landlubbers.

Charlotte Jane's hearty dreams . . .

were rip-roarers!

As the sun came up,
Charlotte Jane
rubbed her eyes.
"Well, blow me down!"

She stretched and somersaulted to her feet.

"Gangway!" she said.

Charlotte Jane peeked in at her parents.
"Juicy sweet dreams, me buckos," she whispered.
It was time to shiver some timbers.

Charlotte Jane the Hearty's *formidable* oomph was back at last.